Shaun the Sheep

Sheep on the Loose
and
Hiccups

EGMONT
We bring stories to life

First published in Great Britain 2009
by Egmont UK Limited
239 Kensington High Street, London W8 6SA

Text by Penny Worms. Based on original storylines by Sarah Ball and
Charles Hodges.

© and ™ Aardman Animations Ltd. 2009. All rights reserved.
Based on a character created by Nick Park. Developed by
Richard (Golly) Goleszowski with Alison Snow and David Fine

ISBN 978 1 4052 4450 3
1 3 5 7 9 10 8 6 4 2

Printed in Italy

FSC
Mixed Sources
Product group from well-managed
forests and other controlled sources
Cert no. TT-COC-002332
www.fsc.org
© 1996 Forest Stewardship Council

Egmont is passionate about helping to preserve the world's remaining ancient forests.
We only use paper from legal and sustainable forest sources.

This book is made from paper certified by the Forestry Stewardship Council (FSC),
an organisation dedicated to promoting responsible management of forest resources.
For more information on the FSC, please visit www.fsc.org. To learn more about
Egmont's sustainable paper policy, please visit www.egmont.co.uk/ethical

Sheep on the Loose
and
Hiccups

2 baa-rilliant stories as seen on TV!

Contents

Sheep on the Loose

Contents

Hiccups

Sheep on the Loose

Adapted from the original episode written by Sarah Ball

Chapter 1
The Great Escape

It was morning on the farm. The sheep were getting restless. They were hungry for their breakfast. Bitzer the dog had overslept and they needed him to let them into the field.

Shaun was very irritated. He had never been happy about having to wait for Bitzer. As if he couldn't cross the road by himself!

When Bitzer finally crawled out of his kennel, he yawned, popped on his little woolly hat and collected his clipboard. He always counted the sheep across the road. He ticked them off like a teacher taking the register.

Bitzer padded over to the gate and looked up and down the road. When he was happy that the coast was clear, he marched through the gate into the road with his clipboard. He stopped in the middle and put his hand up. *Wait for it,* he was saying to the sheep. *It's my job to make absolutely sure it's safe.* Shaun rolled his eyes. *Bitzer can be such a jobsworth at times!* he thought.

Satisfied there was nothing coming, Bitzer signalled to the sheep to cross the road. But before they could move, there was a sudden shriek of brakes. Bitzer whirled round to see a huge double-decker bus bearing down on him. Its driver had slammed on the brakes but the bus was still screeching towards Bitzer. He dropped his clipboard and braced himself, his arms in front of his head. One thought crossed his mind in that split second – *This is it, I'm off to Doggy Heaven*. Bitzer prepared for impact. There was nothing else he could do . . .

SCREEECH! The bus came to a halt centimetres from Bitzer's raised hands. He opened one eye to check that he wasn't dead. Yes, it was all over, and he wasn't dog meat!

Bitzer's relief soon turned to anger. He dropped on to all fours and started barking loudly at the bus driver. Then he started punching the bus, as if he was ready for a fight. Shaun couldn't believe Bitzer was picking a fight with a seven-tonne lump of metal. He looked ridiculous!

The driver was beeping at Bitzer to get out of the road so Shaun decided to put an end to this embarrassing display. He dragged Bitzer away, so the bus could continue down the road. Neither had thought about the flock during this excitement, but when they turned round, their faces fell. Standing in the courtyard, all alone, was Shirley, the biggest sheep in the flock. Where on earth were the rest of them?

Shaun and Bitzer ran out to look down the road. Waving at them from the back of the bus was the flock. They were off on an adventure!

Bitzer looked at the departing bus. Then he looked back at Shirley. Horror of horrors. It dawned on him. He'd lost his sheep! He began to panic. He thrust his clipboard into Shaun's hooves, shoved the whistle into Shaun's mouth and ran down the road waving his arms frantically and whimpering in despair. *Where are those sheep going?*

Shaun looked at Shirley. Shirley looked at Shaun. An understanding passed between them. Shaun had the clipboard and the whistle. He was in charge.

Shaun blew the whistle and pointed to the field. *Breakfast time, Shirley. Off you go.* But Shirley did not move. Shirley did not like to move unless she had to.

Shaun sighed. It seemed there was only one way of getting Shirley into the field. He was going to have to push her.

Shaun put his back into it. It was like pushing a broken-down car, except Shirley didn't have wheels. Her hooves scraped across the tarmac as Shaun shoved her across the road.

Chapter 2
All the Fun of the Fair

A few kilometres away, Bitzer was still running. He'd lost sight of the bus but he couldn't give up. The flock were his responsibility and he had to find them before the Farmer discovered they were missing. He dared not think what the Farmer would do. He might replace Bitzer with a proper sheepdog. He might put Bitzer up for adoption. Worse still, he might put

Bitzer in a home for unwanted dogs. Bitzer imagined it would be full of mean-looking little dogs with big attitudes. He wouldn't stand a chance!

Bitzer stopped by a lamppost to catch his breath. He was starting to hyperventilate. *Calm down*, he told himself. *You'll find them. You have to find them!*

That was when he saw the sign for a funfair. The arrow pointed in the same direction the bus had gone. It suddenly dawned on Bitzer that that was where the bus would stop. And that's where he'd find the sheep! He ran off down the road with renewed energy.

Bitzer was right. The sheep had jumped off the bus at the funfair and were having the time of their lives. They had discovered

Tin Can Alley, a stall where they had to knock down a stack of cans with a wooden ball. The rules were that you could throw the ball three times. If you knocked down the cans, you won a prize. One of the sheep was having a go. His first shot hit the cans, but they didn't topple. His second shot did the same. It was as if the cans were glued together. Suspicious and angry, the sheep took the law into their own hands. Instead of using the little wooden ball for the third shot, the others picked up a sheep and used him as a missile, throwing him over the stall counter. He collided with the cans and they scattered everywhere.

The stallholder was aghast.

The sheep jumped up and down, cheering. They had done it! They had knocked down all the cans! They were going to get a prize!

The stallholder stared at the flock open-mouthed. They couldn't use a flying sheep to knock down the cans. That was cheating! He glared at them.

The flock glared back. They pointed to the prize they wanted – a fluffy pink bunny with a green bow tie and googly eyes. Clearly no other prize would do. The sheep looked so threatening that the stallholder hurriedly gave the fluffy bunny to them. He didn't want any trouble.

Meanwhile, Timmy had troubles of his own. He had become separated from the rest of the flock, drawn to the sweet, delicious smell of a candyfloss maker. Timmy peered over the side of the drum.

Sticky pink fluff appeared magically before his eyes. He watched, mesmerised by the whirring mix and sugary smell . . .

Moments later, the candyfloss man was handing a huge candyfloss to one of the flock. She went to take a bite when suddenly the candyfloss opened a big brown eye, shortly followed by another. *What on earth . . . ?* Shocked, she dropped the candyfloss only to find it wasn't a candyfloss at all, but Timmy covered in the stuff! He had fallen into the drum and had grabbed hold of the candyfloss stick for dear life. Luckily the candyfloss man had pulled him out just in time.

Timmy's mother was cross with him, but Timmy was delighted. He could now look forward to licking himself clean!

Chapter 3

Shaun Pulls the Wool Over
the Farmer's Eyes

Back at the farm, Shaun had managed to push Shirley into the field. He was tired stood panting, while Shirley got on with doing what she did best – eating.

Suddenly, the toilet flushed inside the farmhouse. *Oh, no!* thought Shaun. *The Farmer is awake!* Soon he would look out of the window and discover the empty field. Shaun had to do something or there would be trouble. He needed more sheep, but as the flock had decided to go off on a jolly, he had to come up with some fake ones.

Luckily for Bitzer and the flock, Shaun was not only clever, he was very handy with his hooves. He sawed, he hammered, he painted and he glued, until he'd made the entire flock out of leftover paint and plywood. He ran back to the field and planted the wooden sheep all over the field. And just in the nick of time! The Farmer opened the curtains of the farmhouse and looked out.

There they are, he thought, peering through his thick, smeary spectacles. He marvelled at how sheep could do nothing all day but eat and bleat and there he was with a farm to run.

The Farmer turned away to get his breakfast. He didn't notice Shaun collapse from exhaustion. Poor Shaun. Eating and bleating were very far from his mind. What else was he going to have to do to cover for his wayward friends?

At the funfair, the rest of the flock were laughing their little woolly heads off. Two of the flock had found a big painted cut-out of a sunbathing couple with holes for faces. The two sheep had stuck their heads through, so one looked like a bikini-clad beauty and the other a muscular lifeguard, but with sheep heads! They were pulling funny faces and the rest of the flock were giggling so much it hurt.

Suddenly the laughter faded to silence.

The bathing beauties knew something was wrong but they couldn't see what the other sheep could see . . . It was Bitzer, and he looked cross. The bathing beauties got down. The fun was over.

Shaun would have been relieved to know that Bitzer had found the flock. Shaun knew he couldn't pull the wool over the Farmer's eyes all day. After breakfast, the Farmer would come out and do his chores around the farm. The wooden sheep were only painted on the front. From the back, they were just sheep-shaped planks of wood. The Farmer would certainly find out then.

Shaun was thinking this, when he heard a loud chomping. He looked over at Shirley.

What was she eating now?

What Shirley was eating couldn't have been worse for Shaun. Shirley was taking bites out of all the wooden sheep. Shaun's heart sank. Was there nothing that ewe wouldn't eat?

The situation was desperate. If the Farmer looked out of his window now, he would be horrified. He'd think Shirley had turned into a sheep-munching carnivore! She could be shot on the spot! Of course, Shirley was blissfully unaware of the danger. She burped loudly and carried on, chomping her way through the wooden flock.

Chapter 4

Shaun Has a New Plan

Shaun had to think fast. He didn't have any wood left to make any more sheep. All he had was some leftover paint and he couldn't do a lot with that. Then it dawned on him. He didn't have to! The Farmer's eyesight was so bad that all he was expecting to see were some white fluffy shapes when he looked out of the window. Shaun knew exactly what to do. He darted off to get the paint.

When he came back, he approached the farmhouse like an army commando, flat against the wall, stealthy like a cat.

When he got to the kitchen window, he bobbed up to see the Farmer making a cup of tea and buttering his toast. Shaun knew he would then sit down at the table, right in front of the window. He had only seconds to put his plan into action . . .

Quickly, he dipped the paintbrush into the white paint and dotted some cloud-like shapes on the glass of the window. Then, in a flash, he ducked down again.

Just as Shaun had predicted, the Farmer brought his tea and toast to the table. He peered out the window at his flock. There they were eating and bleating as usual. The Farmer tucked into his toast.

Shaun looked at his watch. Where was Bitzer? He couldn't keep this up for much longer.

Bitzer was at the bus stop outside the funfair, the rest of the flock lined up beside him. They looked even more sheepish than usual. The only cheerful one among them was the large pink bunny they had won on the tin can alley stall.

Bitzer was worried. It was getting late and the Farmer would be finishing breakfast soon. He had to get the flock back before the Farmer noticed.

Shaun was doing such a grand job that the Farmer didn't know anything was wrong. But it was getting quite warm in that kitchen. He needed some fresh air. He went to open the window.

Shaun heard the window slide open above him.

The Farmer looked out.

Uh? The Farmer was puzzled. *Where have those sheep gone?* He could only see the fat one in the middle of the field. He turned around to put his cup away. Shaun bopped up and closed the window again.

When the Farmer turned round, he looked again, unable to believe the sheep had reappeared!

My eyes are playing tricks on me, he thought. But then he noticed that the window had slid shut. He opened it again.

Yikes, no sheep!

There was something odd going on.

Continued on page 21

The Farmer closed the window again and there were the sheep.

Then he opened it – no sheep.

He closed it – sheep.

Opened it – no sheep.

Close – sheep.

Open – no sheep.

Close, open, close . . .

SMASH!

The window glass shattered and the Farmer looked out. There were definitely NO sheep!

Chapter 5
Order is Restored

Shaun knew he had a problem. The Farmer was on his way out of the farmhouse and he didn't have a plan.

Then he heard a vehicle trundling down the lane. It wasn't just *any* vehicle. It was a bright red double-decker bus full of sheep! Bitzer had done it. He'd found the flock and brought them back, just in the nick of time! Shaun ran to the bus and gestured frantically to Bitzer. They needed to get the flock back into the field quickly. But how?

There was only one way – by air.

Bitzer picked up each sheep as it got off the bus and hurled it into the field. Shaun ticked the register as each one landed. If the Farmer could see further than the end of his nose, he would have seen his flock flying into the field. Some landed perfectly, others crash-landed, and little Timmy flew farther than the rest – *Wheeee!* he thought – before he landed on his bottom. Then he was sat upon by the pink stuffed bunny. He disappeared completely under the fluff and fur.

Shaun thrust Bitzer's clipboard into his paws, shoved the whistle into his mouth and ran to join the rest of the flock.

The Farmer came through the gate, grumbling.

Where's that daft dog? If he's asleep in his kennel while my sheep have gone walkabout, there's going to be trouble . . .

But when he looked up, his sheep were right where they should be, in the field, eating and bleating.

Eh? The Farmer squinted just to make sure his eyes weren't playing tricks on him again. Then he jumped. Bitzer had suddenly appeared beside him.

Bitzer thrust the clipboard into the Farmer's hand. The Farmer looked down at the sheep register. Every sheep had a tick. He knew something was out of the ordinary, but he couldn't figure out what. Confused, he turned back to the farmhouse.

Sheep on the Loose

Doggy Heaven, here I come!

The flock waves goodbye from the bus.

The flock tries its luck at Tin Can Alley.

A well-deserved prize.

Shaun works hard to fool the Farmer.

Baa-kini beauty.

The Farmer couldn't believe his eyes.

Shaun is rewarded for a hard day's work.

Hiccups

Shirley gives in to her greed.

Crash, bang, hiccup!

The Farmer tries to regain his balance on top of the ladder.

Timmy gets soaked.

Baa-th time!

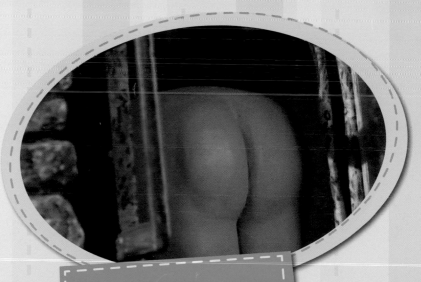

The Farmer's big bare bum!

Bitzer and Shaun congratulate each other,
but perhaps a bit too soon...

...because Shirley's hiccups
seem to have caught on!

Bitzer gave Shaun a thumbs-up and Shaun winked. They'd done it. They were out of trouble. But the Farmer turned round again. There *was* something wrong! There was something pink and fluffy in the field. He looked at it, trying to focus so he could figure out what on earth it was. It looked like a bunny.

Baaa! went the bunny.

The Farmer thought about it for a second. A minute ago there had only been one fat sheep in the field. Now there was one fat sheep, a whole flock of other sheep and a pink stuffed bunny that bleated like a lamb.

Nah! he mumbled. *It can't be.* He decided to go and lie down. It had been a very strange morning.

As the Farmer went back into the farmhouse, little Timmy pushed his way out from under the bunny to find his mummy.

Phew, Shaun let out a big sigh of relief. That was close. Bitzer agreed. And he couldn't have done it without Shaun. He gave Shaun a big toffee apple from the fair to thank him. As Shaun tucked into it, he looked at the pink bunny. A plan started to form in his mind. *The next time that bus rolls down the lane*, he thought, *I am going to get on it*. He smiled his mischievous smile. *Funfair, here I come!*

Hiccups

Adapted from the original episode written by Charles Hodges

Chapter 1
Shirley Gets the Hiccups

Spring had arrived on the farm. The Farmer was up his ladder, giving the farmhouse a fresh coat of paint. Shaun and the flock were in their field, munching on the fresh grass. They were being well behaved for once so Bitzer, the farm dog, decided to make the most of it. He got his picnic table and chair from the shed and set them out in the field. Then he settled down in the sunshine with his latest comic, a bag of crisps and a bottle of pop from the larder. *Ah*, he thought as he let out a long sigh, *life is sweet.*

He nibbled the crisps absent-mindedly while he entered the exciting world of Robo-Dog, The Enforcer. Robo-Dog was Bitzer's favourite comic character – half dog, half robot. Robo-Dog had the super-senses of a bloodhound, but with amazing strength and laser paws. His latest mission was to capture Claws McGraw, a deluded Persian cat and leader of the Mog Mob, who was terrorising the underworld. Claws and the Mob had crushed a sewer-rat uprising and were planning to use the rats and their fleas to unleash a plague on the people of Suburbia. Only one enforcement officer was immune – Robo-Dog was used to flea bites, and if there was one thing he hated more than mustard it was cats!

Bitzer was so engrossed in this latest adventure, that he didn't notice Shirley approaching. And Shirley was hard to miss! She was the biggest, greediest sheep in the flock who would eat just about anything.

Bitzer suddenly heard a slurping sound in his left ear. Puzzled, he looked up, but unlike Robo-Dog, Bitzer wasn't blessed with super-senses. It took him a moment to register that the sound was close. Very close indeed. He turned round sharply to see Shirley with her rubbery sheep lips wrapped around the straw in his pop bottle. She was slurping up the last few drops.

Shirley licked her lips. *Mmm, cherryade.* She was about to start on Bitzer's crisps when he snatched up the bag. He wasn't going to let her steal those as well! Bitzer glared at Shirley, but she just looked back at him innocently. Then she let out a rip-roaring gassy burp right in his face.

Eeugh! Bitzer tried to waft the revolting smell away with his paw. It smelled of soggy grass and rotten fruit, with a tinge of cherry.

Shirley looked at Bitzer, very pleased with herself . . . until she started hiccuping.

That'll teach you, thought Bitzer as he smugly began to eat his crisps again.

Shirley's discomfort grew. She became alarmed at how frequent and violent the hiccups were. And, boy, were they loud!

Chapter 2
Shock Tactics

Shaun was on the other side of the field when he heard the hiccups. He went over to investigate. The rest of the flock turned towards Shirley and Bitzer.

Bitzer shrugged at Shaun. There was nothing he could do about it, was there? It was Shirley's own greedy fault, after all.

Bitzer finished his crisps, but the hiccups continued, and he was starting to get annoyed.

Bitzer thought of a plan.

Shock tactics! That was the way to get rid of hiccups. If he gave Shirley a scare, it was bound to do the trick.

Bitzer blew into his empty crisp packet. It inflated like a balloon. He held the bag in front of Shirley's face and slammed it with his free paw.

POP! It made Shirley jump. Her eyes popped out and her ears flew upright.

Bitzer looked at her.

Shaun looked at her.

Nobody moved.

Had it worked?

Had the hiccups gone?

HIC! went Shirley.

Arggh! went Bitzer. He shook his head. Useless! Greedy sheep.

Shaun was more positive. Maybe a bigger bang would work. He ran off to get an empty feed sack. He brought it back and handed it to Bitzer to blow up.

While Bitzer was huffing and puffing into the large sack, Shaun ran to get a garden fork.

He returned to find Bitzer doing a great job. The sack was almost full of air.

Perfect, thought Shaun. And without hesitation, he stuck the garden fork into the sack.

What a BANG! It shook the whole farmyard like a mini-earthquake.

The Farmer wobbled on his ladder.

The flock was lifted into the air and Shaun was knocked off his feet.

Bitzer, who had been completely

unaware of what Shaun was doing, was frozen to the spot. His eyes were crossed. His mouth was wide open and his skin was stretched back with the force of the blast.

And what of Shirley the incredible hiccuping sheep?

She was still hiccuping.

Right, thought Shaun, not to be defeated. *We need something that makes a noise louder than an inflated feed sack popped by a garden fork.*

As he tried to think music filled his ears. *Where is that coming from?* he thought. Then he remembered the annual rock concert was taking place at the farm next door. An idea began to form . . .

People at the rock concert were amused to see a small flock of sheep walking through the crowds, but nobody thought anything of it. They were in a muddy field after all. It was easy for Shaun and the others to nip backstage, but Shaun knew that getting back out again with a rock guitar and an amplifier wouldn't be so simple so he had organised a distraction. Bitzer was on standby at the cows' gate and as soon as he opened it, the cows stampeded towards the food stalls. As the crowds scattered, Shaun and the others made their escape with the guitar and the amplifier. They would have them back before anyone missed them and Shirley's need was greater and louder than anyone else's.

When they returned, Shirley was still hiccuping. Shaun plugged in the guitar and turned the amplifier up to maximum. It took Bitzer a moment to realise what Shaun was up to, and when he did, it was too late to stop him.

Shaun struck his finest rock star pose and without hesitation, firmly strummed the guitar strings.

KABOOM!

Shaun rocked!

In fact, the whole world rocked!

A ball of fire exploded from the amplifier and the noise was deafening. Up his ladder, the Farmer jumped out of his skin.

The ladder toppled and the Farmer with it. He landed in the pigpen, splattering the Naughty Pigs with mud. They were delighted with the mud shower. The Farmer wasn't so happy. To add to his indignity, the ladder had pulled up a cabbage and it flew through the air and landed on his head.

The Farmer sighed. He had to go and get himself cleaned up.

Chapter 3
Shaun Has a New Idea

Shaun had known that the noise from the amplifier would be loud, but he wasn't expecting an explosion. He looked at Bitzer, who had been caught by the blast. His face was covered in soot and his little woolly hat was singed and smoking.

Shirley looked up guiltily.

Then she hiccuped.

Well, that hadn't done it, thought Shaun. He needed a new plan.

Ah-ha! Suddenly a new idea sprang into Shaun's mind. Bitzer looked worried. He'd already been blasted and blown up. He grabbed hold of Shaun before he could run off, and pleaded with him: *Slowly, carefully, please! No more destruction.*

Shaun nodded. *No problem, Bitzer.* This idea didn't involve noises or scares of any kind. What's the second-best cure for hiccups? Standing on your head for two minutes, of course! The only problem was how to get Shirley upside down. She was so big, it was a job for the entire flock.

On Bitzer's whistle, they got into position, pushing Shirley over to the big tree in the field. *That will hold her up,* they thought.

On Bitzer's second whistle, the strongest sheep began to heave up her bottom so

Shirley rolled on to her head With a big push, they did it. Shirley was standing on her head, supported by the oak tree. All they had to do now was watch and wait.

A few moments passed and no hiccup. The flock started to relax.

A few moments more. No hiccup.

Bitzer looked pleased with himself.

Shirley was beginning to believe it had worked. Maybe she could get down . . .

HIC! Her whole body hiccuped.

The resulting tremor was too much for the oak tree. With all Shirley's weight pushing on the tree, it uprooted and toppled over. Shirley ended up on her back, with her legs flailing like an upside-down beetle, unable to get up again.

And she *still* had the hiccups!

In the farmhouse, the Farmer was putting his muddy clothes in the washing machine. He was grumbling furiously. This wasn't getting the painting done. He stomped upstairs to run a bath so he could get the mud out of his ears and nostrils.

In the field, Shaun was working on a new plan. The next best thing for hiccups, after bangs, blasts and headstands, was drinking water.

He gave Shirley a funnel to hold in her mouth and poured water into it. Shirley gulped and gulped and gulped the water down – a whole bucket full! Shaun put the bucket down. Everyone stared hopefully at Shirley. She remained motionless, the funnel still in her mouth.

The seconds went by. No one moved. They all hoped this was it. Shirley still hadn't hiccupped. The flock started to smile. Yes, it really had worked!

Shaun and Bitzer shook hands. *Good job*! All the sheep cheered.

Shaun took the funnel out of Shirley's mouth. It was a BIG mistake! The water suddenly shot out – a whole bucket full – and Timmy was in the way. The jet of water knocked him off his feet and he landed in a puddle, soaking wet. He hardly knew what had hit him.

And then . . . Shirley hiccuped.

Chapter 4
Bitzer, the Hypnotist

Shaun and Bitzer hung their heads in despair. *Oh, no!* thought Shaun. *Now what?* They had tried bangs, blasts, headstands and water. All a useless waste of time. Maybe they should try something completely different.

Bitzer had seen a man on the television using a clock on a chain to hypnotise people. Just by swinging the clock like a pendulum and speaking in a low, soothing voice, he had made this extremely large, hairy man believe he was a chicken. If hypnosis could have this kind of power over the mind, maybe it was exactly what Shirley needed?

Shaun and Bitzer decided to give it a go. Bitzer swung his whistle in front of Shirley's face just as the hypnotist had done with his clock. Shirley's eyes followed the whistle – left, right, left, right – until her eyelids started to get heavy.

Bitzer waved his fingers and made soothing noises, just as he'd seen the hypnotist do on the television. It worked. Shirley was having trouble keeping her eyelids open. She was drifting into a sleep-like state. Shirley's eyes suddenly became as big as moons. She was hypnotised!

Shaun looked at Bitzer, a big grin crossing his face.

Well I never, thought Bitzer, stunned by his own success. He edged back slowly, away from Shirley. Shaun tiptoed backwards too, watching Shirley carefully. She was still wide-eyed and motionless. Mind over hiccups. That did the trick!

Shaun and Bitzer were so pleased with themselves they high-fived each other. One little clap, that was all it took to break the spell.

Shirley woke up from her hypnotic sleep, and guess what she did? She hiccuped, and it was louder than ever!

Oops, thought Shaun.

Oh, no! thought Bitzer, slapping his hand over his eyes. *What now?*

Chapter 5
The Biggest Shock of All

Meanwhile, in the farmhouse, the Farmer was in his bathroom, wrapped in a towel, getting ready for his bath. His head and hands were still covered in mud and it was getting crusty. The Farmer turned on the taps. *Mmm!* He was looking forward to his bath and feeling clean again.

Outside, Bitzer was trying the very last thing he could think of to rid Shirley of her hiccups and bring peace and quiet to the farm. If bangs, blasts, headstands, water *and* hypnosis had all failed, there was only one thing left. She had to hold her breath for as long as possible.

Come on, girl, Bitzer mumbled encouragingly. *You can do it.* So Shirley took a deep, deep breath and held it.

Bitzer tapped his watch. He'd let her know when she could breath out.

Shirley nodded in agreement and Bitzer strolled off to join Shaun, who was chuckling over Bitzer's comic. He had found a comic strip called Born Dippy about a sheepdog who was so daft that the sheep followed him around just to see what silly thing he would do next. When Bitzer joined him, they began to read it together. Their chuckles turned to giggles. Their giggles turned to laughter. Meanwhile Shirley's face got bluer and her eyes began to bulge. Bitzer had totally forgotten about her.

Upstairs in the farmhouse the Farmer's bath was ready. All he needed was his little yellow ducky. He picked up the duck, but it slipped out of his hands.

Aw! the Farmer moaned. *I'll have to get that myself then*, he grumbled.

He bent down to pick up the duck and his towel slipped off. He suddenly felt the cold air from the open window hit his bare behind. It was a shock, but not as much of a shock as it was for poor Shirley. Forgotten about by Bitzer, her brain was being starved of oxygen, her eyes were bulging out of her head. And just when she thought her discomfort couldn't get any worse, she saw the most gruesome sight in the history of sheepkind – a big, bare, baggy bottom glaring at her from the open window. It was horrible!

Shirley screamed.

The flock screamed.

Timmy's mother covered his eyes.

Shaun and Bitzer turned to see what was causing all the commotion. They recoiled in disgust, covering their own eyes from the sight at the bathroom window.

The Farmer stood up, unaware of his audience below, or their reaction. He popped his ducky in the bath and climbed in, sinking down into the hot water.

Shaun carefully took his hands away from his eyes. Had that ugly thing gone?

Bitzer opened his eyes too. The flock were wide-eyed and frozen to the spot. Timmy was twitching. *Poor lamb*, thought Bitzer. He was about to click his fingers in an attempt to get the sheep out of their state of shock, when Shaun tapped him on the shoulder.

Look over there, Bitzer! Shaun gestured. *What do you think?*

Bitzer turned to look at Shirley, who gulped down a mouthful of grass. There seemed nothing wrong with her now. She was as greedy as ever.

Bitzer sighed with relief and shook Shaun's hoof. *At last!* he thought. Peace had finally been restored to the farm. Bitzer was happy in that thought for at least two seconds . . . until Timmy started to hiccup.

Bitzer whirled round to look at him.

Not again! he thought. *Please, not again!*

But it got worse. Timmy's mother started to hiccup. Before long, the whole flock was hiccuping, and it was all down to the shock of seeing the Farmer's bare behind. Shirley looked up and smiled. She was fine.

Bitzer stood in the middle of the field and howled. What on earth was he going to do now?

WIN WIN WIN!

100s of Shaun the Sheep prizes to be won online!

We're **giving away** Shaun the Sheep books, Nintendo DS games, DVDs, posters, mobile phone skins, charms, toys and much more online.

Remember: ewe have to be in it to **win** it!

*Terms and conditions apply.
Full terms online at
www.egmont.co.uk/shaunthesheepcompetition

Aardman © Aardman Animation Ltd 2009

To get your hooves on one of these
sheep-tastic prizes, simply log onto
www.egmont.co.uk/shaunthesheepcompetition
and enter!